That Moment In Time

One: I'll Never Forget It

J.R. Whitsell

Copyright © 2020 J.R. Whitsell
All rights reserved. No part of this book may be reproduced or used in any manner without the written permission of the copyright owner except for the use of quotations in a book review. For more information: JR Whitsell PO Box 196 Canyon, TX 79105 jrwhitsellauthor@gmail.com.

This is a work of fiction. Names, characters, places, and incidents either are the product of the author's imagination or are used fictitiously. Any resemblance to actual persons, living or dead, events, or locales is entirely coincidental.

ISBN: 979-8-6830-9482-9 (paperback)
Imprint: Independently published

DEDICATION

To Dad—I miss you.

PREFACE

As of 2020, over 50 million people have dementia worldwide, according to the World Health Organization[1].

The following short story is a work of fiction based on real experiences. For over a year, my mom, my wife, and I cared for my dad, whose dementia had reached late-stage.

Our goal was to keep Dad at home and out of an assisted-living facility as long as possible. Caregiving two weeks on, two weeks off, my wife and I split time with Mom.

I journal everything, and I noted every experience, symptom, and emotion with my dad. My desire is to describe dementia and caregiving through a series of short stories.

Before my dad lost his mind, I thought memory loss was the definition of dementia. What I knew was far from the truth. Dementia is a horrible disease that profoundly affects the patient and their loved ones.

Dementia—in all its forms—makes life miserable

for the patient and caregiver. Caregiving isn't a one-person job, and as the patient's symptoms advance, help is imperative. There are resources, support groups, and in-home respite nurses available. I encourage anyone dealing with a loved one stricken with dementia to research and utilize the help in your community.

---

1. Dementia. (2020). Retrieved 5 September 2020, from
https://www.who.int/news-room/fact-sheets/detail/dementia#:~:text=Rates%20of%20dementia,is%20between%205%2D8%25

ACKNOWLEDGMENTS

Thank you to all the nurses and staff who take care of our loved ones with dementia.

I know your job is beyond difficult. You are the professionals who take over when the family can no longer do the work.

To all the caregivers—hang in there. Caregiving may be the hardest thing you ever do. It is worth it.

1

At The Home

When Phyllis tilted her head back to swallow the oval, white pill, Mary swiped the plastic medicine cup and put it in her shirt pocket. Freakin' kleptos, I swear everyone with dementia is a damn thief.

I sat on a sofa that smelled like disinfectant with a hint of urine in one of the common areas at Green Oaks Memory Care. The name of the joint is just another example of a business trend I've noticed. Over the past ten years, stores, restaurants, salons, real estate developments, and (apparently) old folks' homes are branded by combining a single adjective with a noun. I suppose Green Oaks is more inviting than Pencey Housing for the Chronically Confused. It's like my favorite coffee shop—Aromatic Bean. It might be less popular if it were named Overly Priced Addictive Liquids. However, by implication, that name would work as well.

My only entertainment was the two ladies who absolutely hated each other but hung out as if they were best friends.

"You need to go outside and leave me alone," Mary snapped at Phyllis.

"Oh, shut up," Phyllis said as she shook her head in disgust.

Then Mary started shaking her head too. Then the duo turned away from each other in their chairs, and both shook their heads with repugnance.

Kimberly, one of Dad's nurses, told me she needed to finish getting him ready, and they would meet me in a few minutes. In other words, Dad crapped his pants. So, Kimberly and at least one other nurse were showering, diapering, and dressing Dad. Don't get me wrong, I appreciated how the staff delicately danced around the reality of late-stage dementia. But after fourteen months of showers and diapers, incontinence—front or back—was no big deal. The three of us—my wife, Cindy, my mom, Diane, and me—were seasoned veteran caregivers.

I reclined on the sofa and crossed my legs. There was a bulge at the bottom of my jeans, near my right ankle. The bulge was soft, and when I lifted my pants leg, I realized it was a dirty sock. I started to push the sock up toward my calf to keep it hidden. Then no one would know I had grabbed the jeans out of the bottom of the hamper that morning. But I didn't really care, so I pulled the sock out and stuffed it in my pocket. After taking care of Dad for so long, things like wearing dirty jeans and t-shirts from the late '90s became common. I had to prioritize everything in my life, and laundry was low on the list.

"Mr. Gallaher," a woman said, approaching from my right. It was Marie, my father's physical therapist. In her mid-twenties, with dark hair, perfect skin, and an ever-present smile, Marie spent an hour a week with Dad. Her job was to redevelop the motor skills he'd lost due to his sick brain. She had a just-out-of-college belief that she could reignite the minds of the memory-impaired. Her optimism was borderline annoying.

"Marie, please call me Pax," I said.

"Hi Pax, how's your dad today?"

"I haven't seen him yet. Kimberly is dressing him. We haven't talked in a week or two. How's he doing?"

"We've made progress with a few things," Marie replied. She opened my dad's folder to review the condition of his executive function. "He was able to tie a few knots for me last week until he got distracted. And we're still trying to work through the remote-control issue."

"Marie, I appreciate it, but there are two televisions in the common areas. So I don't think it's necessary or even possible for him to control the one in his room." I was trying my best to be respectful of

Marie's goals to help Dad relearn skills that I knew he never would.

"Pax, I think your dad can make improvements in several areas, but I need some help from you and the rest of the family," Marie said as she sat in the chair next to me. "It's all about consistency and routines if we're going to get where we want to be."

"Marie, with all due respect, please don't talk to me about routines. I quit my job and drove school buses to make ends meet so I could live a life of routines with Dad," I responded with an edge in my voice.

"I know you did, Pax. I just think that if we are all on the same page and consistent with all our interactions with Phil, you'll be surprised at what he can achieve."

"Marie, when I was caregiving for Dad, we had five daily routines. Each of the five consisted of specific steps."

"Pax, I know you did a terrific job—"

"Let me tell you what the morning routine

was," I said, interrupting Marie. "I got out of bed at 4:30, and I would almost always find Phil sitting on the couch staring into space. I would tell him good morning and start the coffee protocol, which consisted of six steps. Now, we had built a coffee bar so that everything we needed was in one spot. This made the coffee protocol more manageable."

"Pax," Marie said with a nervous tone.

"Hold on, let me finish. The first step was to retrieve the creamer from the refrigerator and bring it to the coffee bar, so it was under my control. I would pour the creamer into two coffee cups and put it back in the fridge. If I didn't put it up, Phil would grab it, and we'd have cream-filled plates, bowls, and pans.

"Like I said, I had the water, coffee, filters, and coffee maker all in the same spot to make our javas as Phil stood, six inches behind my right shoulder. I would make Phil's coffee first, keeping an eye on him with my peripheral vision. Otherwise, he would mess with anything on the kitchen counter.

"I would hand Phil his coffee before I started

making mine. I had to stand between Phil and the coffee maker or trust me there would be a messy, potentially dangerous disaster."

"Pax," Marie tried to interject.

"This won't take long. Then I took my coffee to the living room, sat on the couch, and turned on the television. Eventually, Phil would join me on the couch.

"After his attention was on the television, I would slip back to the kitchen. I'd get his meds from the locked cabinet and take the five pills and a cup of water to Phil. I used the same blue cup, which I cleaned every morning and evening.

"To get Phil to take his pills, I had to follow these steps exactly: First, I took the coffee cup from Phil and moved anything near him that might be distracting. Second, I put the meds in Phil's right hand and placed the water cup in his left hand. Third, I would say, 'Down the hatch.' I actually had to say that. On a good day, it worked the first go around."

I placed my hand on the arm of Marie's chair to make sure that she was still listening. "I'm almost done," I continued.

"Then, I returned to the kitchen to make breakfast. Since Phil was right behind me again, I continued monitoring his actions to prevent him from grabbing raw bacon or a hot skillet.

"I placed Phil's plate on the table to encourage him to sit. I made sure he followed me all the way to his chair at the head of the table. Otherwise, he would stay at the stove and eat from the pan.

"Once he sat and began to eat, I would pour him some milk or juice. Then I made my plate and sat at the table with him. Occasionally, Dad would wander off, which required me to coax him back to his breakfast.

"After we ate, I would take our plates, silverware, and glasses to the sink to rinse and put into the dishwasher. I couldn't leave the dirty dishes in the sink, or Dad would take them to his bedroom. Again, He was right behind me while I washed the plates and flatware.

"All total, there were twenty steps to the

morning routine. Every day, along with four others, we followed the same patterns," I concluded my monologue. I looked at Marie with a smug face that suggested she shouldn't tell me how to care for my father.

"I know it was hard on you. Most people wouldn't do all of that. I will keep you updated on his progress," Marie said, maintaining a professional facade. But she was pissed. She stood, made her way toward the exit, and scanned her identification, which opened the secure doors.

All in all, my interaction with Marie was one of my better conversations in the past few months. The combination of homebound isolation and the emotional exhaustion of watching my father's decline had significantly affected my social skills. It had been five weeks since we moved Phil into Green Oaks. I hadn't had time to jump back into friendships or interacting with people in general.

"There's Pax over there," Kimberly said.

I looked to my left and saw Dad shuffling toward me with a familiar grin. He recognized me but had no clue I was his son. His gray beard had grown long, and his eyes were more sunken than I remember from the last time I saw him.

Kimberly guided him by his right arm, trying not to force his movements. She led Dad to the chair that was vacated by Marie. Though it was apparent that Kimberly wanted Dad to sit, he'd lost the ability to infer.

"Hey," Phil said, his usual rote greeting.

"Well, hello, Phil Gallaher. How are you?" I asked. Opinions vary on how to interact with dementia patients and what may confuse or make them nervous. I didn't feel comfortable calling him Dad at the beginning of a conversation. I figured surprising him with a son he didn't know would be counterproductive. But, at late-stage, Phil knew little more than his own name.

I was still sitting, hoping my dad would naturally sit down to visit. But dementia made him antsy, and getting him to sit down was always a chore.

"Can you sit down, Phil?" Kimberly asked.

"Mm-hmm," Phil said, still standing.

"Okay, let's sit down then," Kimberly persisted and gently tugged his arm toward the chair.

"Oh, well...I was...you know," Phil said as he continued to resist.

After a minute or so, Phil finally gave in and sat down. I thanked Kimberly, and she left to attend to a disagreement that had gotten out of control between Phyllis and Mary.

"How are you feeling today," I asked.

"Well, I was just thinkin' about...those guys said they might be here, but I don't know," Dad said. His language had declined to confused sentence fragments over the past six months.

"You know that day you taught me how to drive? That was something," I said, starting the conversation with the first topic that popped in my head. I avoided the phrase 'remember when,' which experts claim causes aggravation.

"Mm-hmm," Dad agreed.

"You had that Chevy pick-up with the extended cab, which was a big deal back in 1983."

"Yeah, it was pretty good for…you know…"

"It sure was a nice truck. It was much better than the one I have now. Mine is so bad the birds in the neighbor's tree won't stop crapping on it," I said with a laugh.

Dad mirrored me and faked a laugh.

"But I was only eleven, and you let me drive your truck down that dirt road like I had a clue what I was doing. Of course, I didn't," I said.

"Oh boy," Dad said with a chuckle.

"When I got to the first turn, I thought I was supposed to speed up, not slow down. So, I floored it. Then you yelled out, 'Whoa Pax, whoa,' and I hit the brakes before we drove into the mesquite trees," I said as I laughed and slapped Dad gently on the knee.

"Yeah, you didn't know what you had goin' till you got goin', then you did."

"That's true. I almost forgot about that. But I remember exactly what you said to me when I got to the blacktop, just before we switched seats."

"Oh, you do?" Dad asked.

"You said, 'Hey Paxle Grease,' you called me that back then. I looked you in the eyes, and you said, 'I'm proud of you.' Dang, what a great day," I said with genuine enthusiasm.

"Well, I guess I better go see," Dad said as he stood from his chair.

"I didn't mean to run you off. Do you want to go to your room?"

"Yeah"

Dad followed me back to his room and to his recliner. I turned on his television and changed the channels until I found a western movie. Dad had always loved westerns. But for the past few months, there wasn't much that kept his attention.

Dad sat in his recliner and started slapping his right hand with his left. He was really banging away, which meant he was anxious about the conversation, or maybe he couldn't remember who I was. I figured I should leave before he became more agitated.

"Well, I better get going," I said once it was apparent that Dad's mind had drifted.

"Mm-hmm," he said as he attempted to untie

the knots from the string that Marie had left in his recliner.

"Anyway, happy birthday. Mom made you a cake. We'll celebrate this weekend," I said as I stepped toward the door.

"Oh, I see."

"Alright, see you in a little bit," I said, knowing it would be more than a little bit.

2

I was on the couch when Cindy got home around 5:30. She looked tired from another long day counting the beans for Coffee, Watson & Dodd, CPAs.

"Hey," I said as both of our terriers ran across the living room to greet my wife.

"Hey. How was your visit with your dad?' Cindy asked.

"It was fine."

"Just fine?"

"I mean, you know…fine," I said.

"I'll change, then we can talk," Cindy said as she headed to our bedroom.

"Alright. I was about to wash my truck, knock off a layer of bird crap, but it can wait," I babbled. I got up and went to the backyard, where we usually visited.

Cindy changed into a t-shirt and shorts and joined me in the shade of our pergola. I was staring at the trumpet vines on our fence. Occasionally one of some fifty bees surrounding the plants darted inside a red flower to mine for nectar.

Between our chairs was a table where Dad had neatly placed several of his "treasures." The tabletop was covered with golf balls and poker chips—Phil's entertainment while living with us.

Usually, the pergola provided significant relief from the sun. But with the temperature approaching one-hundred degrees, there was no escaping the heat.

"I'm so ready for the fall," I said.

"Me too. Even for Texas, this is too hot."

"Yeah, I always look forward to the fall this time of year," I said as I wiped the sweat off my forehead with a napkin from my pocket that read

PenceyBurger in kelly green lettering.

"Didn't eat lunch at Green Oaks today?" Cindy asked.

"I didn't feel like dealing with Phyllis and Mary's drama."

"I understand. Man, those two hate each other."

"But there's a problem with wishing for the cool of the fall because of summer heat," I said, circling back to our weather discussion.

"Alright, I'll bite. What's the problem?" Cindy asked as one of the terriers, Bandit, jumped into her lap.

"Well, if you spend the summer imagining the fall, you'll miss so many good things. Of course, that's obvious. I mean, we were married in the summer, the vacations with the kids, and things like sitting here on the porch together," I said as I fiddled with one of the poker chips. "Think about it, wasn't it yesterday when we were teenagers?"

Cindy was fifty-two, and I was forty-eight. Despite our efforts to stay in shape, we both felt the limits that middle age brought.

"I don't feel like a teenager. But yes, I agree that life is short," Cindy said, sliding a strand of brunette hair from her eyes with her finger. "Are you thinking about the time you missed with your dad before all this?"

"I don't have regrets when it comes to Dad. Everything happened the way it happened. That's life," I said, tossing the poker chip back onto the table.

"But that leads me to the real problem, which isn't as obvious. It's not as superficial as hoping for a future that is better than our present," I said. I paused, making sure Cindy was keeping up with my rabbit-trail thoughts.

"Go ahead," Cindy said.

"I mean, if we see our lives as one human experience after another, we completely dismiss the parts that make up the whole. We have such little regard for the life and death of the cells that make those moments happen," I said. I waited—mid-rabbit trail—for Cindy to process what I was trying to say.

"Dead cells?" Cindy raised an eyebrow.

"You know how our bodies are made of trillions of cells? We wouldn't be who or what we are if it weren't for all of those cells," I continued.

"Yeah."

"Well, billions of our cells die daily. They work together to give us life, and then they're gone. The way I see it, those cells sacrificed themselves so we could have that moment in time. If we ignore that moment anticipating something better, then we're saying our present cells aren't as valuable as future cells."

"You're crazy, Gallaher," Cindy said, grinning and squinting from the sunlight.

"I know, but you get it. Which makes you crazy too."

"I suppose that's true. And I love you, so I must be crazy."

"I love you too, even in this convection oven air," I replied. I leaned over and kissed Cindy's lips.

"I'm worried about you, Pax," Cindy said.

"Why?"

"You've never forgiven your dad for his drinking problem. You blame alcoholism as the cause of his dementia when you don't know that to be true. You go on and on about the birds crapping on your truck, but you don't park somewhere else. You've never talked to the neighbors about getting rid of the birds. It's like you want to stay miserable," Cindy replied.

"Cindy, you're an accountant, so I know you're not metaphorically saying the shit on my truck is really my resentment of life's circumstances," I said, shaking my head at her rare poetic insight. "But, when I try to remember my dad before his drinking got bad, it's difficult. And that scares the hell out of me. What if I'm only left with the memories of the years just before he detoxed? When he was drinking screwdrivers for breakfast." I covered my mouth with my hand. I hadn't let those thoughts escape before that point.

"Pax, it's up to you, but I think you should take some time and try to remember the good memories of your dad. I know you can. Also, you have to forgive him, or you'll carry that anger around forever. Sit down with him and tell him you forgive him because he drank too much."

"Tell him that? Cindy, my dad is almost catatonic. What difference does it make if I tell him I forgive him?" I asked with an edge to my voice.

"It's not for him. It's for you. I know in my heart that you will be better off if you tell him face to face that you forgive him," Cindy said, looking at me with sympathetic green eyes while she held my hand.

"Alright, then that's what I'll do," I said, knowing she was right again, which irritated the hell out of me.

"I'm not letting you off the hook that easily," Cindy said. She wanted me to open up and tell her what was eating at me and had made me bitter.

"I don't know what you want me to say. Yes, I'm mad, and I don't know if I should be."

"What makes you so mad?"

"Well, you've read the same books that I have about dementia. Do any of them definitively state what causes it?" I asked.

"No, other than theories and contributing factors, they haven't figured out the cause."

"So, the cause isn't known. But according to the book that Mom has, we shouldn't blame the patient. Because the disease wasn't caused by something the patient did, they get a pass on their life decisions," I said in a slightly louder voice.

"Take it easy, Pax. Yes, I read that too."

"Well, is it just me, or is there flawed logic there?" I scoffed. "Doctors don't know the cause, but they tell you not to blame the dementia patient. Well, maybe alcohol caused his dementia. Maybe dementia caused the alcoholism. The two might be mutually exclusive. But excuse me if I get a little emotional about the whole damn thing," I said. Tears were beginning to well in the bottom of my eyes. I attempted to wipe them away with the sweat-soaked PenceyBurger napkin.

Cindy got out of her chair and knelt with her head in my lap, hugging my waist. "You're right. Alcoholism may have caused this, maybe not. But either way, what difference does it make, Pax?"

"I just miss my dad. I want my dad back, dammit," I wailed as I folded over my wife, embracing her while we both wept.

3

Dad's seventy-second birthday party was more like a five-year-old's, complete with balloons and party hats.

Attendees inside the Green Oaks private dining room—Cindy and me, our three children with their spouses, and Mom—sat around the large table wearing cone hats. Mom removed the foil from Dad's favorite chocolate cake, which she baked the night before. Dad's eyes danced when Mom cut and served him a large piece of the German Chocolate dessert.

We talked for about an hour, took pictures, and posted a few on social media for Dad's brothers and friends to see.

When Dad started pacing around the room while slapping one hand with the other, I told Mom that I would take him back to his room. She gave Dad a kiss, told him that she loved him, and wished him one last happy birthday.

Dad followed me through the security door into the common area, and I asked if he wanted to sit down for a minute.

"Yeah," he said. Then, much to my surprise, he sat on the couch.

I sat in the chair next to him and thought about what I had already rehearsed in my head. "Dad, I need to tell you something," I began.

"Mm-hmm," Dad responded.

"I've been angry at you for some time because of how your drinking got out of control. I got so obsessed with how alcohol took over your life that I started to forget all the great experiences we had together," I said.

A memory of Dad and I fishing for trout unexpectedly flashed through my mind. I was a teen, and Dad had taken off early from work to take me to a nearby pond.

"Well...I was thinkin' that..."

"Yeah, so anyway, I want you to know I forgive you for the drinking. Also, I had no right to judge you. It's not like I haven't had and still have my own issues," I continued.

I started to remember the details of the day we went fishing. I recalled how the two of us whooped while angling the feisty fish.

"Anyway, you made me into the man I am, and I will always love you," I said through a lump in my throat.

"I need to check on...over there," Dad said as he stood and started to walk to his room. So much for any emotional father-son moment.

I got up and followed Dad to his room. I had said what I needed to say. Now I hoped I could move past the anger that haunted me.

Dad walked into his room and turned around to close the door before I could enter. Apparently, I didn't have to worry about how I said goodbye.

I turned around and headed toward the window to ask Patricia to press the buzzer to let me out. Just as the automatic lock clicked open, I heard Dad.

"Hey," he said as he stood with the door open just enough that I could see his face.

"Yeah, Dad, what's wrong?" I asked.

"I'm proud of you," Dad said and closed the door.

4

Cindy was waiting for me in the parking lot when I exited Green Oaks. The rest of the family had already left.

"Well, how did that go?" she asked.

"Let's go get some real food and talk about it," I suggested.

We got in the car, and I drove us through downtown Pencey. The city revitalized the area several years ago, but the brick roads and nineteenth-century storefronts were still intact, preserving the Americana feel. Inside the stores, restaurants, and the coffee shop, the square's quaintness transformed into modern convenience. Every business had wireless internet, ambient music, and top-notch air conditioning.

I parked in front of our favorite restaurant, Savory Essence—see, adjective-noun—and we walked through a wrought-iron gate to sit on the patio. The outdoor dining at Savory Essence is well shaded with large fans that provide enough air circulation to negate the summer heat.

After the waiter gave us menus and two glasses of water, Cindy anxiously asked again. "So, did you talk to him?"

"Yes. I did what you recommended, and I forgave Dad. I also apologized for judging him the way I have," I said. I waited for Cindy to pry the rest of the story out of me.

"Oh, come on. Are you going to make me beg? What happened?" Cindy asked. I think she was excited to hear if I felt better and, more importantly, if she had been right.

"Well, your idea was a good one, I suppose," I said. "While I forgave Dad, I remembered a day when he came home early from work so we could go fishing."

"When was this?"

"I think I was probably fifteen. Someone told Dad about this pond stocked with trout, and you know how much he liked to fish. I've never been crazy about fishing, but he was so excited when he picked me up," I said, smiling. "We caught our limit in less than ten minutes. But it wasn't about fishing. I was happy because Dad wanted to spend time with me. That was a memory I thought I would never forget, but I nearly did."

"That's great, honey. Of course, you know what this means," Cindy said.

"Yes. You told me so, and I'm glad you did. Thank you,"

"You're welcome. Also, think about all the cells that made today's moment and the one of your fishing trip possible," Cindy quipped.

"Oh, I'm way ahead of you. I've already told the cells how much I appreciated them today. Said a little prayer for the ones that already died," I replied.

"How about you say a little prayer for us,"

Cindy said. She placed her hand on the table, palm up.

I took my wife's hand, and we bowed our heads. I thanked God for all the experiences we had with Dad, the ones we still had with family and friends, and the moments to come. Cindy and I prayed together at the ceramic tile-top table, the sound of the bar's blender, diners' chatter, and Bossa Nova music in the background.

We ate dinner and talked about all we'd been through taking care of Dad. We were happy for the time that he was in our home. Even in bad times, there are blessings if you look for them.

We discussed what might happen in the future, but we didn't dwell on it too long. The cells that would create that reality didn't exist, and we didn't want to neglect the ones making our present.

5

Cindy was waiting for me in the parking lot when I exited Green Oaks. The rest of the family had already left.

"Well, how did that go?" she asked.

"Let's go get some real food and talk about it," I suggested.

We got in the car, and I drove us through downtown Pencey. The city revitalized the area several years ago, but the brick roads and nineteenth-century storefronts were still intact, preserving the Americana feel. Inside the stores, restaurants, and the coffee shop, the square's quaintness transformed into modern convenience. Every business had wireless internet, ambient music, and top-notch air conditioning.

I parked in front of our favorite restaurant, Savory Essence—see, adjective-noun—and we walked through a wrought-iron gate to sit on the patio. The outdoor dining at Savory Essence is well shaded with large fans that provide enough air circulation to negate the summer heat.

After the waiter gave us menus and two glasses of water, Cindy anxiously asked again. "So, did you talk to him?"

"Yes. I did what you recommended, and I forgave Dad. I also apologized for judging him the way I have," I said. I waited for Cindy to pry the rest of the story out of me.

"Oh, come on. Are you going to make me beg? What happened?" Cindy asked. I think she was excited to hear if I felt better and, more importantly, if she had been right.

"Well, your idea was a good one, I suppose," I said. "While I forgave Dad, I remembered a day when he came home early from work so we could go fishing."

"When was this?"

"I think I was probably fifteen. Someone told Dad about this pond stocked with trout, and you know how much he liked to fish. I've never been crazy about fishing, but he was so excited when he picked me up," I said, smiling. "We caught our limit in less than ten minutes. But it wasn't about fishing. I was happy because Dad wanted to spend time with me. That was a memory I thought I would never forget, but I nearly did."

"That's great, honey. Of course, you know what this means," Cindy said.

"Yes. You told me so, and I'm glad you did. Thank you,"

"You're welcome. Also, think about all the cells that made today's moment and the one of your fishing trip possible," Cindy quipped.

"Oh, I'm way ahead of you. I've already told the cells how much I appreciated them today. Said a little prayer for the ones that already died," I replied.

"How about you say a little prayer for us,"

Cindy said. She placed her hand on the table, palm up.

I took my wife's hand, and we bowed our heads. I thanked God for all the experiences we had with Dad, the ones we still had with family and friends, and the moments to come. Cindy and I prayed together at the ceramic tile-top table, the sound of the bar's blender, diners' chatter, and Bossa Nova music in the background.

We ate dinner and talked about all we'd been through taking care of Dad. We were happy for the time that he was in our home. Even in bad times, there are blessings if you look for them.

We discussed what might happen in the future, but we didn't dwell on it too long. The cells that would create that reality didn't exist, and we didn't want to neglect the ones making our present.

ABOUT THE AUTHOR

J.R. Whitsell, MBA, spent 25 years as a marketing and development professional for global corporations and small start-ups.

Over his lifetime, J.R. has been a corporate vice-president, a founder of companies and entities, and a leader in multiple civic/religious organizations. Never content, J.R. also has a class A CDL and drives buses and tractor-trailers for his community's local school district.

J.R.'s father began showing signs of dementia in 2013. By 2019, his symptoms were consistent with late-stage. J.R, his mother, and his wife--cared for the family patriarch from 2018-2020.

He lives in Northwest Texas with his wife, Sara.

@jr_whitsell   jrwhitsellauthor@gmail.com

Other Works By

J.R. Whitsell

That Moment In Time – Two: What If We Helped?

That Moment In Time – Three: Something Is Really Wrong

His Other Life: A Novel

Made in the USA
Monee, IL
21 January 2022